Being Jessica Isn't Easy.

Elizabeth picked up her books and went to the door. Now she was really in bad shape. She had two things to do this afternoon—Mr. Davis's detention and decorating the gym. How was she going to manage both? And how was she going to handle the Unicorns? If Lila Fowler had her way, Elizabeth would be doing the special job they'd been saving up for Jessica. What a mess! And it was all because of the past success of their great April Fools' Day joke. Now, no matter how many times she told the truth, everybody still insisted that she was Jessica pretending *to be Elizabeth!*

Bantam Skylark Books in the SWEET VALLEY TWINS series
Ask your bookseller for the books you have missed.

Sweet Valley Twins Super Editions

SWEET VALLEY TWINS

April Fool!

Written by
Jamie Suzanne

Created by
FRANCINE PASCAL

A BANTAM SKYLARK BOOK®
TORONTO • NEW YORK • LONDON • SYDNEY • AUCKLAND

RL 4, 008–012

APRIL FOOL!

A Bantam Skylark Book / April 1989

Conceived by Francine Pascal

Produced by Daniel Weiss Associates, Inc.,
27 West 20th Street,
New York, NY 10011

Cover art by James Mathewuse

ISBN 0-553-15688-8

Published simultaneously in the United States and Canada

PRINTED IN THE UNITED STATES OF AMERICA

O   0 9 8 7 6 5 4 3 2 1

To
Jordan David Adler

One

◇

Elizabeth Wakefield was perched comfortably on a broad, low limb of the enormous pine tree in the Wakefields' backyard. She had pulled her knees up under her chin and her back was propped against the pine tree's sturdy trunk. This was Elizabeth's "thinking seat," the place where she always went to be alone when she had some serious thinking to do.

There was a lot to think about. Tomorrow, Mr. Davis, the sixth-grade homeroom teacher, had promised that he would announce the winner of the class essay contest. Elizabeth had written about saving the whales. She felt confident that her essay stood a very good chance of winning the prize, a year's free subscription to the winner's favorite magazine.

Elizabeth frowned thoughtfully and hugged her knees. Should she subscribe to *The Horse Lover's Journal* or to *Mysteries From Around the World*? She loved horses and took riding lessons at Carson Stable. But she loved reading mysteries, too, especially those of Amanda Howard, and she was getting pretty good at figuring out who had committed the crime before the detective solved it. She decided she would subscribe to *Mysteries* now, and ask for *Horse Lover's Journal* for her birthday.

But there was another reason Elizabeth was looking forward to tomorrow, and the thought of it brought a gleam to her eyes. It was the first of April—April Fools' Day—the day that she and her twin sister, Jessica, played their annual April Fools' Day joke. It was their tradition to switch identities. They had played the joke so many times that no one was fooled anymore, but still it was a lot of fun.

Elizabeth and Jessica were identical twins. They had the same long sun-streaked, blond hair, sparkling blue-green eyes, and a deepset dimple in their left cheeks. They wore exactly the same size, and were equally tanned from hours of play in the California sunshine.

But that's where the similarities ended. Although the twins looked exactly alike, their personalities and interests were worlds apart. Elizabeth was older than Jessica by four minutes, but sometimes it seemed more like four years. Elizabeth was the serious one. She loved to read and devoted a lot of time to writing for *The Sweet Valley Sixers*, the class newspaper. She also liked to spend time alone, just thinking. The "thinking seat," where she was curled up now, was her favorite spot. When they were younger, Jessica had shared the secret meeting place with Elizabeth, but now she thought she was far too busy and too mature to spend any time there.

Jessica preferred passing the time with the Unicorns, an exclusive group of the most popular and snobbiest girls at Sweet Valley Middle School. The group spent a lot of time chattering about makeup, clothes, and boys. When Jessica wasn't with them, it usually meant that she was at home having one of her marathon telephone conversations with them.

The twins had just recently stopped dressing alike. Jessica's taste ran to short skirts and

bright-colored tops; she especially loved purple, the color of royalty and the official color
of the Unicorns. Elizabeth dressed more con-
servatively. And whereas Jessica wore makeup
on her peaches-and-cream complexion, Elizabeth liked the natural, well-scrubbed look. She
usually fastened her gleaming hair back on
each side with barrettes or pulled it into a
sleek ponytail. Jessica wore her hair down in
loose waves around her shoulders.

On April Fools' Day, when the two girls
switched identities, it was always a big change—
especially for Elizabeth, who was more sensi-
tive to the differences between them. She had
been looking forward to the switch, until Jessica had mentioned that she had a much better idea for their April Fools' joke this year—an
"absolutely, positively, *great* idea." Elizabeth
was skeptical since she knew that Jessica's
ideas usually led to trouble. In fact, Elizabeth
usually wound up having to bail Jessica out of
the trouble she got everyone into. But, she
was still waiting eagerly for Jessica to come
home and tell her what she had in mind.

When Elizabeth looked up and saw Jessica
skipping across the lawn with a wide smile on
her face, she waved and moved over on the

limb to make room for her twin. "Hi, Jess!" she called. "I wondered when you'd be getting home. I was thinking about tomorrow."

"I was, too," Jessica said breathlessly, swinging one leg over the limb and straddling it. "I've been thinking about it all day! My new idea is *so* terrific that no one will be able to figure it out!"

Elizabeth laughed. "This had better be good, Jess. We already *have* an April Fools' joke that everybody thinks is terrific. Everybody's already counting on us to switch."

"But that's the problem, Lizzie," Jessica said. "All our friends *expect* us to switch."

"So what if they do?" Elizabeth leaned back against the trunk of the old pine. "It's still a good joke, isn't it?"

"Yes, but I've got a *better* one," Jessica cried, her cheeks pink with excitement. "We won't actually change identities, we'll just *pretend* that we have!"

"What?" Elizabeth gave her sister a puzzled stare. "Jess, have you flipped? What do you mean, 'pretend' to change?"

"It's simple, really," Jessica said. "We won't switch, but we'll emphasize all our differences. I'll wear my wildest outfit, even more makeup than usual, and lots of my favorite perfume. Everybody will think I'm you, pretending to be me. And you can wear your most conservative clothes and your plainest hairstyle, and everybody will think you're *me*, pretending to be you. Get it? It's not the switch everyone's waiting for. It's a *non-switch*."

Elizabeth wrinkled her forehead. "I think I get it," she said doubtfully. "But won't everyone be totally confused—including *us*?"

"But we *want* everybody to be confused!" Jessica exclaimed gleefully. "They'll think I'm Elizabeth, and they'll think you're Jess. No matter how often we tell them they're wrong, I'll bet they won't believe us! And at the party after school tomorrow, we can tell everybody what we've done. It'll be a *terrific* April Fools' joke! Even our teachers and our best friends will be fooled, and maybe even Mom, Dad, and Steven."

Elizabeth tried to imagine how people would react to what Jessica was proposing. "You know, Jess," she said slowly, "I think you're right. Everybody *is* expecting us to switch. And when we don't, they'll be completely fooled."

Jessica slid off the limb onto the ground.

"You mean you'll do it? That's great!" She gave Elizabeth a big hug and began to giggle. "Oh, Lizzie, I can't *wait* for tomorrow night's party. Just think of the look on everybody's face when they realize how badly they've been fooled!"

Elizabeth giggled, too. "I have to hand it to you, Jess," she said admiringly. "It's just crazy enough to work." She paused. "So what are you going to wear?"

Jessica thought for a moment. "Maybe my short denim skirt with the hearts on the pocket. A blue top—no, I think my hot-pink T-shirt is better, don't you? My pink sneakers with a pair of pink-and-yellow socks. And lots of jewelry."

Elizabeth laughed as she pictured the attention her twin was sure to attract with her colorful outfit. Jessica liked nothing better than to have people notice her. "It's definitely *Jessica*, all right," she said.

Jessica giggled again. "It's so absolutely Jessica that everybody will be convinced that it's Elizabeth *pretending* to be Jessica!"

Elizabeth put her hand to her forehead. "Oh, stop," she begged with an exaggerated moan, "you're making my head spin! In a minute,

I'll forget who's supposed to be who! I'll be seeing double.''

Jessica jumped up and down. "Exactly!" she cried triumphantly. "That's exactly the idea! We want everybody to be so confused that they think they're seeing double!"

Elizabeth nodded. "I'll wear my red-and-white gingham blouse," she said. "And my—"

"Oh, Lizzie," Jessica interrupted. "There's something I have to tell Mom before I forget. I'll be right back, and we can finish planning what we're going to wear."

As her sister darted across the lawn, Elizabeth settled back down onto the tree limb. It was going to be fun *not* being Jessica for a day, especially when everybody was sure to think that was exactly who she was. For once, her twin had come up with a sure-fire plan. This was going to be an April Fools' joke that their friends and family would never forget!

Two

"Hey!" came a shout and a loud bang on the bathroom door. "Whoever's in there, hurry up! I have to brush my teeth or I'm going to be late!"

Elizabeth grinned to herself in the mirror as she smoothed back her golden hair and fastened her barrettes. Her older brother Steven would have to wait. He was going to be the first victim of their wonderful April Fools' joke. Elizabeth wore her gingham blouse with her favorite jeweled horse pin, a pair of neatly-pressed jeans, and sneakers. A copy of one of Amanda Howard's mysteries was tucked into her back pocket.

"It's just me, Steven," she called, in an extra-sweet voice. "Elizabeth. I'm hurrying as fast as I can." She opened the door. "Happy April first," she said, in her most Elizabeth-like voice. "The bathroom's all yours now."

His fist raised for another bang, Steven stared at her suspiciously. Then he grinned. "You mean Happy April Fools' Day, don't you, *Jess*?"

Elizabeth shook her head, feeling the laughter bubbling up inside her. Score one! They'd fooled Steven! "But I'm *not* Jess," she said happily. "I'm Elizabeth."

"And I'm the man in the moon."

"But it's absolutely *true*!" Elizabeth exclaimed earnestly. "Cross my heart and hope to die!"

"Heart?" Suddenly Steven grimaced and clutched his chest. "Heart?" he moaned, leaning against the wall for support.

"What's the matter, Steven?" Elizabeth asked uncertainly. Her brother was such a clown that it was hard to know when he was playing or when he was serious.

Steven was doubled over. "Oh, please, Jess, call an ambulance!" he groaned. "I think I'm having a *heart* attack!"

Elizabeth stared at her brother. "You're fooling, aren't you, Steven?" she asked anxiously.

"I'm *not* fooling, honest, Jess," Steven moaned. "It's my heart—it hurts!" His lips twitched and he slid weakly down the wall and onto the floor. "Quick! Dial 911! I need a doctor!"

April Fool or no, Elizabeth couldn't run the risk of something happening to her brother. She ran to the top of the stairs. "Mom!" she cried, "Dad! Steven's sick!"

"April Fool!" Steven chortled, jumping to his feet. He grinned. "Boy, did I get *you* going, Jess!"

With dignity, Elizabeth turned around and lifted her chin. "I am *not* Jess," she said.

The bathroom door slammed and Steven whirled around. "Hey! I'm next!" he protested.

"But I was next *first*!" Jessica's light, teasing laugh came through the door.

"Rats," Steven muttered. "If you don't hurry up, Elizabeth, I'm going to come in and *drag* you out!"

When Jessica finally emerged from the bathroom, Elizabeth couldn't help laughing. Her twin was wearing the outfit she had planned— a denim miniskirt, a hot-pink T-shirt, pink sneakers, and pink-and-yellow socks. Her lips and cheeks were pinker than usual, and her blue-green eyes sparkled mischievously.

Steven brushed past her into the bathroom. He suddenly put his hands to his throat and made a gargling noise. "Don't you think you've overdone Jessica's perfume, *Elizabeth*?" he choked out.

Elizabeth sniffed. Jessica was wearing just a shade too much of her favorite Wild Rose perfume. It was the perfect finishing touch.

"Jess," she whispered as they went down the stairs together, "you look *terrific*!"

Jessica pushed her wavy hair back from her face. "So do you," she said admiringly. "That horse pin you're wearing is perfect. Well, we fooled Steven—let's go see what happens with Mom and Dad."

With a laugh, Elizabeth skipped into the kitchen where her mother was pulling a plate of melon slices out of the refrigerator.

"Good morning, girls," Mrs. Wakefield said cheerfully.

Jessica gawked. "Mom!" she exclaimed. "Your hair! It's . . . it's red!"

Mrs. Wakefield smiled at Jessica and patted her bright red hair. "Do you like it, Elizabeth?

I colored it last night. Don't you think it's lovely?"

Elizabeth didn't think her mother's new red hair coloring was at *all* lovely, but she didn't want to hurt her feelings. She liked the gold color that was so much like her own. But Jessica wasn't thinking of her mother's hair color.

"Wait a minute," she objected, trying not to smile. "You've got us confused. That's Elizabeth over there, *I'm* Jessica."

"She's telling the truth, Mom," Elizabeth added, sitting down at the table.

"Of *course* you're telling the truth," Mrs. Wakefield said soothingly. She wiped her hands on her apron and turned to Jessica. "Would you mind setting the table for breakfast, dear?"

"But it's *her* turn," Jessica said, pushing out her lip in an exaggerated pout and pointing to her twin. "I set the table last night!"

Elizabeth jumped up hastily, with a wink at her sister. "I'll be *glad* to do it, Mom."

"You see!" Mrs. Wakefield said triumphantly. "You *have* changed places! Jessica, you're playing Elizabeth's helpful role. And Elizabeth, you're pretending to skip out on your chores, just the way Jessica always does. You girls can't April Fool me! I know both of you too well.''

Elizabeth and Jessica exchanged mischievous grins. Their trick was working exactly the way they had planned it!

At that moment, Mr. Wakefield came into the room, wearing a business suit and a tie. He put his briefcase down beside the table and went to the window. "Good morning, everybody," he said happily, looking out at the golden California sunshine. "Isn't it a simply beautiful spring day?"

"Dad!" Elizabeth cried, pulling him around. "Your tie! You've got it on backward!"

Mr. Wakefield looked down. "Why, you're right! *My* tie *is* on backward." His brown eyes glinted merrily and he gave his wife a kiss without even seeming to notice her bright red hair.

"Daddy, you're crazy!" Jessica exclaimed.

"April Fool!" Mr. Wakefield cried.

The twins giggled.

"Aren't you overlooking something, Ned?" Mrs. Wakefield asked. "Something very new and different?" She came up beside him and patted her red hair coyly. "Something exciting?"

"Am *I* overlooking something?" Mr. Wakefield said, casting a glance at Elizabeth and Jessica. "Why, yes," he said, still ignoring Mrs. Wakefield's new hair color. "I believe I *am* overlooking something, after all. I believe the twins are backwards, too."

He smiled at Elizabeth. "Good morning, Jessica." He turned to Jessica with an elaborate little bow. "And how are you this morning, Elizabeth?"

Elizabeth and Jessica giggled at one another. "We are *not* backwards!" they announced together. "We're *ourselves!*"

"I'm Elizabeth," Elizabeth said. "As usual."

"And I'm Jessica!" Jessica exclaimed. "Exactly the way I always am."

"And *I'm* wearing a wig," their mother crowed, pulling it off and shaking out her own lovely golden hair. "I didn't change the color of my hair! I'm exactly the way I always am, too. April Fool, everybody!"

While Jessica laughed and her father chuckled, Elizabeth burst into helpless giggles. April Fools' Day was only an hour old, and she'd been taken in three times already: once by Steven's fake heart attack, once by her mother's bright red wig, and once by her father's backward tie. But the best joke of all was on her family because they hadn't figured out that the twins were only pretending to have switched places.

"Isn't this great?" Jessica asked happily, as the girls collected their books after breakfast and started off down the driveway. "They all fell for our joke. They were expecting us to switch, so they thought that's what we'd done. Our plan is working perfectly!"

Elizabeth nodded in agreement. They certainly *had* fallen for it. "I only hope that our joke goes over as well at school as it did at home!"

Three

As the twins walked toward their homeroom, April Fools' Day was in full swing. Jim Sturbridge, wearing a plastic Groucho Marx nose and moustache, was greeting everybody at the door. Next to him, Ricky Capaldo was shaking everybody's hand.

"Oh, yuck!" Elizabeth exclaimed as she pulled back her hand from Ricky's grip and made a face. "My fingers are all gooey!" Beside her, Jessica grinned and put both hands behind her back.

Looking at Elizabeth, Ricky laughed. "Happy April Fools' Day, *Jessica!*"

"But I'm Elizabeth," Elizabeth said, taking out a tissue to wipe her hands. "Can't you see what I'm wearing?"

"Sure we can see," Jerry McAllister said knowingly, coming up to Elizabeth and Jessica with a camera. "But today's the day of the famous twin switch, isn't it?" He grinned at Jessica and pointed his camera at her. "How about a picture, Elizabeth?"

"Sure," Jessica replied happily, "except that I'm Jessica, not Elizabeth." She looked into the camera with a flirtatious smile.

Jerry pushed a button on the camera and a squirt of water hit Jessica's cheek. "Got'cha!" he shouted. "April Fool!"

"That's not very funny, Jerry," Jessica complained.

"Oh, come on, Jess. Don't be such a bad sport," Elizabeth said, laughing. She pulled out a tissue and handed it to her twin. Just then, somebody tapped Elizabeth on the shoulder. She turned around to see Lila Fowler, one of Jessica's best friends, scowling at her.

"You're not wearing anything purple today, Jessica," Lila snapped. "Aren't you proud to be a Unicorn?"

Elizabeth shrugged. "I'm not wearing purple because I'm *not* a Unicorn." Elizabeth thought the Unicorns were snobbish, but she didn't say that out loud. "I'm Elizabeth, not Jessica."

But Lila wasn't paying any attention. She leaned forward, her thick, light brown hair falling over her shoulders. "Jessica," she said, as if she were giving a lecture, "some of the girls are complaining that you've been neglecting the Unicorns lately. They think that you haven't been doing your part on some of our projects."

Elizabeth raised her eyebrows in surprise.

Lila continued without giving her a chance to respond. "Anyway, don't forget about the Unicorns' project this afternoon," she commanded. "We're saving a special job just for you. We're meeting right after school by the front entrance, so don't be late."

"A special job?" Elizabeth asked. "This afternoon?" She shook her head. "Sorry, but you'll have to let *Jessica* know about that. She's the one you want. *I've* got to help decorate the gym for tonight's party."

"Ha-ha," Lila said. "Don't try to pull that tired old April Fools' joke on me, Jessica Wakefield. We all know that *Elizabeth* is the one who's doing the decorating." Lila stuck her nose in the air and flounced away.

"Ss-ss-t," somebody hissed. "Mr. Davis is coming!" They all scrambled for their seats as the homeroom teacher came into the room.

"Good morning, class," Mr. Davis said, walking briskly to his desk. He smiled at them.

"Good morning, Mr. Davis," the class chanted loudly.

Mr. Davis bent over and looked at something that was sitting on the corner of his desk. "What's this?" he asked, picking it up. "An apple for the teacher? How thoughtful!"

In the corner of the room, Charlie Cashman snickered.

Mr. Davis turned the apple in his hand. There was a note attached to it. " 'To our teacher,' " he read aloud, " 'with love from Winston Egbert.' "

"But I didn't—" Winston sputtered, the tips of his ears turning bright red. Elizabeth was sure that Winston hadn't put the apple on Mr. Davis's desk. He was too shy to call attention to himself.

Mr. Davis was smiling. "Thank you, Winston," he said warmly. "It's nice to know that somebody appreciates—" But then he broke off, staring at the apple. It had come apart in his hands, and there was a fat green-and-yellow plastic worm in the hollow middle.

A ripple of laughter went around the room. In the front row, one of the girls cried, "Oh, gross!" And from the back corner, Jerry McAllister called "April Fool!" The ripple became a wave as everybody joined in the laughter, including Elizabeth and Jessica. Mr. Davis had certainly been fooled!

"April Fool, eh?" Mr. Davis said, giving them all a stern look. "All right, then, we'll see who's got the last laugh." He pulled a stack of paper out of his desk drawer and began to hand out sheets. "Pencils, everybody. We're having a pop quiz."

There was a general groan. Everybody hated Mr. Davis's pop quizzes.

"OK." Mr. Davis looked around with a scowl on his face. "Here's your first question. How far can a bear run into the woods?"

The entire class stared at Mr. Davis with their mouths open.

"Don't gawk," Mr. Davis said severely. "And don't giggle. Just write the answer."

Elizabeth nibbled her pencil, thinking. She *loved* to solve puzzles. But this one was hard—

and very tricky. When you thought about it carefully, you could see where the trick was. A bear could only run halfway *into* the woods, couldn't it? After that, it was running *out* of the woods. It seemed like a dumb answer, but she decided to write it down anyway. To her surprise, her pencil slid smoothly over the surface of the paper without making a single mark!

Behind her, Jim Sturbridge gasped, "Hey! My pencil won't work!"

"Why, this paper isn't paper at all!" Nora Mercandy exclaimed, holding her piece up to the light. "It's *plastic*!"

"April fool!" Mr. Davis announced with a twinkle in his eye.

When the giggles quieted down, Mr. Davis continued. "Let's move on to something equally important. Today we find out who won the essay contest. Is everybody ready?"

"Ready," the class called out. Elizabeth squirmed, taking a deep breath. Everybody always said that she was the best writer in the class, and she had put hours of work into her essay.

Mr. Davis made a big show of opening his desk drawer, pulling out a sealed envelope, and tearing it open. "The winner—" he announced, in a deep, important voice, "is Elizabeth Wakefield, who wrote an essay on saving the whales!"

Elizabeth let her breath out in a delighted little whoosh. Then she started to push her chair away from her desk and stand up. But as she did, she was startled to see that Mr. Davis was looking toward the other side of the room, where *Jessica* was sitting!

"Come on, *Elizabeth*," he said, motioning Jessica to the front. "Come up and get your award—a year's subscription to your favorite magazine."

With a glance at Elizabeth, Jessica started to object. "But I'm not—"

Mr. Davis shook his head. "We all know about the famous April Fools' twin switch that you two girls pull every year. You might be able to fool some people, but you can't fool me. *You're* really Elizabeth, and your twin over there"—he jerked his thumb in Elizabeth's direction—"is really Jessica. So come on up and get your award, *Elizabeth*."

Jessica giggled. "Well, OK, Mr. Davis."

With a big sigh and a what-else-can-I-do look at her twin, Jessica got up from her desk and marched to the front of the classroom. Elizabeth watched in helpless frustration as Jessica accepted the award *she* had earned for writing the best essay!

But the worst was yet to come. After he'd shaken Jessica's hand and congratulated her, Mr. Davis unfolded a piece of paper and picked up his pen. "Now," he said expectantly, "what magazine would you like to subscribe to, Elizabeth?"

Elizabeth waited, holding her breath. Last night, she'd told Jessica how hard it had been to decide between the mystery magazine and *The Horse Lover's Journal.* She hoped that Jessica would remember that she had decided to get the mystery magazine.

Jessica thought for a minute, looking down at the form on Mr. Davis's desk. Then she looked up and said, "I'd like to subscribe to *Teen Rock!*"

Teen Rock! Elizabeth glared at Jessica. How *could* she? But then, as the class began to laugh, Elizabeth understood what had happened. Jessica was only going along with their April Fools' joke—she was Jessica being *Jessica.* And as a result, everybody was convinced that she was really *Elizabeth* being Jessica. She shook her head helplessly. Maybe tomorrow morning she could talk the whole thing over with Mr. Davis and convince him to change the subscription.

With a puzzled look at Jessica, Mr. Davis scratched his head. "Well, Elizabeth, I have to say that I think you're carrying your April Fools' joke just a little too far. But if that's the magazine you want, then that's what you'll get." He finished writing, folded the form, put it into an envelope, and licked the flap. "I'm mailing this today so you get your first issue as soon as possible."

Today! Elizabeth felt a wave of disappointment sweep over her. That meant she couldn't change the subscription after all! She was stuck with a full year of *Teen Rock*, Jessica's favorite magazine! She bit her lip and slid down into her seat. Maybe this April Fools' joke wasn't such a terrific idea after all.

Four

◇

"Hey, Jessica," Pamela Jacobson called out after the bell ending class had rung. "I just have to tell you that I think your April Fools' joke is really great. You look *exactly* like Elizabeth! And what's more, you act like her, too. Really you ought to be an actress." She giggled and pointed to the Amanda Howard mystery sticking out of Elizabeth's pocket. "Everybody knows how much Elizabeth loves mysteries! That Amanda Howard book is really a nice touch."

Elizabeth laughed gaily. "But you've got it

all mixed up, Pamela," she said. "I *am* Elizabeth. Really and truly."

"But that can't be. If you're Elizabeth, how come *you* didn't go up to get your award?" Pamela pushed her wavy brown hair out of her eyes and lifted her chin. "No, you can't convince me, Jessica. That award was really important to Elizabeth, and I'm glad she got it. Congratulations on a great joke!"

With a delighted laugh, Elizabeth gathered her books and turned to go. She couldn't be angry with Jessica. After all, the magazine subscription wasn't as important as knowing that her essay had been the very best. And Jessica had really been right about their April Fools' joke. Their family, their friends, even their teachers—everybody was *completely* confused by their non-switch. What a great day!

As she was leaving the classroom, Mr. Davis called out to her. "Jessica, I need to talk to you. Please come up to the desk." There was a sharp edge to his voice.

With a little frown, Elizabeth turned around. "Actually, Mr. Davis," she said earnestly, "I'm really Elizabeth. I'm not Jessica at all. If it's important, you ought to talk to her."

"Look, Jessica," Mr. Davis said shortly, "I

know who you really are, and I want to talk to *you*, not to your twin."

Elizabeth heaved a sigh and approached Mr. Davis's desk. He took something out of the bottom drawer. His face looked stern, and there were frown wrinkles between his eyebrows.

"Sit down, Jessica," Mr. Davis said. "We have to talk about something."

Elizabeth sat down in one of the front seats, a feeling of apprehension beginning to mount inside her. Mr. Davis held up a piece of lilac-colored notepaper with a pink rose in one corner. Elizabeth recognized it immediately as the notepaper Jessica had gotten for her birthday. Even from her seat she could smell the sweet scent of lilacs on the piece of paper.

Mr. Davis was watching her. "Ah," he said with satisfaction, "I see that you recognize this notepaper. That's true, isn't it?"

"Yes," Elizabeth admitted, biting her lip. "It's Jessica's notepaper."

Mr. Davis's frown deepened. "You mean, it's *your* notepaper, don't you? And I'm sure you must recognize the handwriting as yours, too. Nobody else in the class dots all their i's with little round circles, the way you do, Jessica."

Elizabeth sighed again and her shoulders drooped. If Mr. Davis insisted on believing that the paper was hers, there wasn't much she could do about it.

"Well, then, since you admit that the handwriting is yours, maybe you'll want to hear what you wrote," Mr. Davis continued. He looked down at the lilac paper and began to read out loud. " 'Dear Lila, Isn't that green shirt Mr. Davis is wearing simply *awful*? And can you believe that he's wearing it with a *purple* tie? Yuck! That man has *no* taste!' "

Mr. Davis put down the note and looked at Elizabeth. "What do you have to say for yourself, Jessica? What do you think about what you've written?"

Elizabeth gulped. She knew that Jessica sometimes liked to poke fun at her teachers, but this was really too much. She opened her mouth to protest that *she* hadn't written it, but then she closed it again. If she confessed the truth now, their best-ever April Fools' joke would be spoiled. She'd feel like a traitor to Jessica. Anyway, Mr. Davis might not believe her story. He seemed absolutely convinced that she was Jessica pretending to be Elizabeth. No, there wasn't anything to do but give Mr. Davis exactly what he wanted to hear—an apology.

Mr. Davis was still waiting, impatiently drumming his fingers on his desk. "Well?" he demanded, frowning. "Don't you have *anything* to say?"

Elizabeth swallowed hard. "I'm really sorry, Mr. Davis," she said in a sincere voice. "I'll never do anything like this again. Never, ever," she added for good measure.

Mr. Davis's frown deepened to a scowl. "But that's exactly what you said last week when I intercepted the note you wrote to Ellen Riteman about Lois Waller's weight problem," he said, still drumming his fingers. "Do you remember our discussion on that occasion?"

Elizabeth chewed her lip. Of course she didn't remember. But she couldn't tell Mr. Davis that.

Mr. Davis leaned forward, crossing his arms on his desk. "I'm afraid," he said with a sigh, "that a simple apology just isn't good enough this time, Jessica."

Elizabeth sucked in her breath. "It isn't?"

she asked apprehensively. What did Mr. Davis have in mind?

Mr. Davis shook his head. "No, it isn't. Before you leave my sixth-grade class at the end of this year, you simply *must* learn the importance of respecting other people's feelings. Therefore, I'm going to ask you to write an essay on that subject. And to make sure that your essay is done properly—and that *you* do it, without any help from your twin—I want you to come to this classroom immediately after school today. And bring plenty of notepaper and pencils."

"After school?" Elizabeth burst out. "But I can't! I'm helping to decorate the gym for the April Fools' party tonight!"

Mr. Davis shook his head sadly. "Jessica, I wish you'd stop falling back on that silly April Fools' joke. I happen to know that Elizabeth is involved with the party decorations, not you. Now, don't forget. Be here promptly after the last bell. The earlier you get started writing your essay, the earlier you'll be able to finish. Then you can feed the gerbils."

"Yes, sir," Elizabeth sighed. If she hadn't felt so frustrated, she would have laughed at Mr. Davis's last instruction. Jessica hated feeding the gerbils. She considered them dirty, noisy little creatures, and she never saw anything amusing in their antics. It was the worst punishment Mr. Davis could think up—worse even than writing an essay. If she were really Jessica, she'd be horrified at the thought.

Elizabeth picked up her books and went to the door. Now she was really in bad shape. She had two things to do this afternoon—Mr. Davis's detention and decorating the gym. How was she going to manage both? And how was she going to handle the Unicorns? If Lila Fowler had her way, Elizabeth would be doing the special job they'd been saving up for Jessica. What a mess!

As Elizabeth went out into the hall, the humor of the situation suddenly struck her and she began to giggle. It was true things were very mixed up and she had lots of obligations to fulfill later in the day. But it was all because of the success of their great April Fools' joke. No matter how many times she told the truth, everybody still insisted that she was Jessica *pretending* to be Elizabeth! Not counting the detention, things were working perfectly! She couldn't wait to tell Jessica when she saw her in cooking class.

Suddenly, Elizabeth realized that the hallway was empty. She looked up at the clock over the lockers. It was five past! She was already five minutes late to cooking class, and Mrs. Gerhart was very strict about promptness. She should have gotten a late pass from Mr. Davis. Without it, she was really going to be in trouble.

Elizabeth quickened her step, remembering the school rule about not running in the hallway. But after all, she *was* terribly late, and there wasn't anybody around to bump into.

Elizabeth hurried even more. She was walking *very* fast when she rounded the hallway corner, and smacked right into Mr. Edwards, the vice principal!

Five

◇

"Elizabeth Wakefield!" Mr. Edwards said sternly. "I'm *shocked* to see you, of all people, running in the hall! You know the rule, don't you? And what are you doing here, anyway? You're supposed to be in class!"

Elizabeth was tongue-tied. All she could do was try not to show how breathless she was.

Then a strange look came over Mr. Edwards's face, and he smiled a sly, knowing smile. "Ah, yes," he said, stepping back and looking Elizabeth over from head to toe. "Today is April Fools' Day, isn't it? And you're not Elizabeth Wakefield at all. You're *Jessica* Wakefield."

Elizabeth shook her head. "No, sir," she said, "I—"

But Mr. Edwards didn't give her time to finish. "Well, then, since you're Jessica, this business makes a little more sense." He stared down at her. "Didn't we talk just last week about the importance of walking *slowly* down the hall, rather than skipping or running?"

Elizabeth cleared her throat. "But I—" she began.

"Well, then, I think this matter calls for some kind of more serious punishment," Mr. Edwards said. "There's quite a lot of filing to be done in my office. I'll expect you today after school, for an hour or so, to help out my secretary, Mrs. Peters."

Elizabeth's mouth flew open. "Today?" she squeaked. "But I couldn't possibly—"

Mr. Edwards looked down his nose at her. "Do you have a late pass?"

Elizabeth shook her head.

"Well, then," Mr. Edwards sighed, "I suppose I'd better give you one." He pulled a pad of pink passes out of his pocket, scribbled on the top one, and tore it off with a flourish.

"Here you are, Jessica," he said. "And no more running. Understand?"

Elizabeth nodded.

"Very good." Mr. Edwards turned and went off down the hall, his heels clicking smartly against the polished tile.

Elizabeth stared down at the pass in her hand, not sure whether to laugh or cry. She'd been wishing for a late pass, and now she had one—even if it was in her sister's name. But she also had another detention! What a *crazy* morning this was turning out to be!

Mrs. Gerhart's cooking class was taught in a room equipped with six small kitchens, each with its own stove, sink, cabinets, and counter. Jessica was already in her kitchen, putting on a red-and-white checked apron.

"Where have you been?" Jessica whispered nervously, as Elizabeth put her books down on the counter. "Mrs. Gerhart already checked the roll. She thinks I'm you. And she put down an absent by *my* name!"

"Well, then, you're safe," Elizabeth said, with a wry grin. "I've got a late pass, so she'll have to erase the absence. But I've also got two detentions—and one of them is yours!"

Jessica stared at her twin, her eyes widening. "Two detentions!" she exclaimed loudly. Then she threw a hasty glance around to see if Lila had heard her, and began to whisper. "Two detentions?" she hissed. "How did you do that? And what do you mean, one of them is mine?"

Elizabeth explained what had happened with Mr. Davis, and then what had happened with Mr. Edwards. "So I've got two detentions," she finished up. "And Lila thinks I'm supposed to help the Unicorns with one of their projects." She shook her head. "How am I going to make it to the gym to help decorate for the party? What a mess!"

Jessica was grinning broadly. "No, it's *great*!" she exclaimed. "We're fooling everybody! Don't you see how *perfect* everything is?"

Elizabeth got her blue apron out of her drawer and put it on. "Well, you're not the one who has to serve two detentions."

Jessica gave her a sympathetic look. "I'm sorry you're having a hard time, Elizabeth." She tugged on a lock of her blond hair, frowning a little. "Do you think we ought to call it quits and let everybody in on the joke?"

Elizabeth stared at her twin. "Hey, Jessica,"

she cautioned in a teasing voice. "Aren't you acting out of character?"

"No, really, Lizzie. I mean it. It sounds as if things are sort of piling up on you. If you want me to, I'll go take Mr. Davis's detention." She made a face. "It really *is* mine, anyway. After all, I was the one who wrote that stupid note."

For a minute, Elizabeth was tempted. If Jessica would take Mr. Davis's detention, that would solve only part of the problem. It would also ruin their joke.

She straightened her shoulders. "No," she whispered firmly. "It's OK. Let's stick with it. Our joke is better than anything anybody's ever done."

Jessica flashed her a grateful smile. "Are you sure, Lizzie?"

Elizabeth nodded. "And anyway, people might not believe us if we told them the truth!" She gave Jessica a mock stern glance. "But listen, try to stay out of trouble for the rest of today, will you? I don't think I could handle *another* detention!"

Jessica grinned. "I promise to be good." She glanced over her shoulder. "Here comes Nora with our eggs. We can't talk any more."

"Eggs?" Elizabeth asked, as Nora gave Jessica and Elizabeth four eggs each, and then went off to her own kitchen, adjoining theirs. "What are we making today?"

"Today, Jessica," Mrs. Gerhart said, coming up behind Elizabeth, "we are making a soufflé. If you'd been on time, you would have heard my instructions. But no doubt you were off somewhere, playing another April Fools' joke."

"No, I wasn't," Elizabeth said, "I was talking to Mr. Davis and—"

Mrs. Gerhart smiled at Elizabeth. "If you want to know the truth, Jessica, if I had a twin, I'm sure I'd switch places with her on April Fools' Day, too. So it doesn't matter to me that you're cooking in Elizabeth's kitchen or wearing her blue apron. I'll play along with your game because I know exactly who both of you *really* are!"

"But we *haven't* sw—" Elizabeth started to say. Then she bit her lip. At least Mrs. Gerhart wasn't angry at her. She nodded. "Yes, ma'am."

Mrs. Gerhart smiled. "Now, do you have your pass?"

"Here it is." Elizabeth held out the late pass

Mr. Edwards had given her, with Jessica's name written on it.

Mrs. Gerhart took the pass, opened her grade book, and made a notation next to Jessica's name. "The recipe for the soufflé is on the blackboard, Jessica," she said, closing her book. "Remember, a soufflé is very delicate. You have to measure all of the ingredients *exactly* and you have to be especially careful when you cook it. If you underbake it, or if you bang the oven door when you look at it, it's likely to fall."

Elizabeth nodded, listening attentively. Today, of all days, she couldn't afford to mess up. Hard as it was going to be, she had to get her soufflé just right.

And it *was* hard, especially with Jessica giggling noisily with Nora. Jessica was so inattentive that she splattered two eggs onto the floor. Then her hand slipped and the cheese she was grating ended up in the sink.

"What a pain!" Jessica sighed. "*Elizabeth*, I don't understand how you can always be so neat." She turned to Nora. "Look, Nora. See how neat *Elizabeth's* kitchen looks."

Falling in with the joke, Nora nodded.

"You're right. *Elizabeth* is the neatest person I know."

"And she's like that at home, too," Jessica continued loudly. "Her room is as neat as a pin, with everything organized, right down to her last pair of shoes." Jessica was really playing her role to the hilt.

Elizabeth, meanwhile, was doing her best not to let Jessica's antics distract her. Following the recipe on the blackboard, she measured the flour and milk and grated cheese carefully into a small pan and stirred the sauce while it was cooking to make sure it didn't burn. Her sauce came out perfectly golden and creamy-smooth.

While Jessica was excitedly telling Nora what she was going to wear to the next Johnny Buck concert, she carelessly dumped all her ingredients together and stirred the sauce only a couple of times. The result was a scorched and lumpy mess that tasted too salty.

And while Elizabeth was slowly and carefully folding the stiffly-beaten egg whites into her cooked sauce, being careful to incorporate as much air into the batter as possible, Jessica was relating to Nora the sentimental saga of one of her favorite soap operas and munching on a handful of grated cheese. Folding in the egg whites was something that Jessica couldn't be bothered with, so she just dumped them in and stirred them around for a little while.

In forty minutes, Elizabeth's soufflé was ready to come out of the oven. She opened the door carefully and peeked in. Yes, it was ready, and it was perfect—high and light and golden, just like the picture Mrs. Gerhart had shown them. Using hot pads, she had just put it safely on the counter, out of the draft, when she heard a loud BANG! Guiltily, Jessica looked up from the stove. "I guess I closed the door a little too hard," she said innocently.

When Jessica's soufflé came out of the oven, it was heavy as a brick, with a brown, leathery crust. There was a deep, sunken pit in the middle of it. Jessica stared at the mess for a minute, then sighed noisily and threw up both her hands.

"I'll *never* get the hang of cooking," she exclaimed dramatically. "Never. No matter how hard I try!"

In the adjoining kitchen, Nora started to giggle. "Oh, Elizabeth," she laughed, tossing her long dark hair over her shoulder, "you are too much! You're playing Jessica perfectly!

Somebody ought to nominate you for best actress!"

"Well, Elizabeth," Mrs. Gerhart said, coming into the kitchen and staring at Jessica's disastrous soufflé. "Perhaps you *should* get an acting award. But one thing's certain—nobody's going to nominate you for any cooking awards!" She frowned. "I'm surprised at you. Usually you do a much better job than this." She took out her grade book and ran her finger down the list until she came to Elizabeth's name. "I don't think I can give your effort much more than a C."

Elizabeth stepped forward. "Oh, but wait!" she exclaimed, as Mrs. Gerhart's pen was poised over her grade book. She pointed to the perfectly golden soufflé on the counter. "*This* is my soufflé!"

Mrs. Gerhart beamed. "And what a beautiful soufflé it is!" she exclaimed. "Jessica, it looks simply scrumptious!" With a fork, she took a tiny bite of it and rolled her eyes in delight. "Mm-mm. And it tastes every bit as good as it looks! Jessica, I'm so pleased! This is your very best effort so far this year!"

Still beaming, Mrs. Gerhart ran her finger down the list until she came to Jessica's name.

She wrote an A next to it. Next to Elizabeth's name, she wrote a C.

Dazed, Elizabeth stared at the grade book. She'd never before gotten a C in Mrs. Gerhart's class. It wasn't fair!

But there wasn't a single thing she could do about it. Mrs. Gerhart really believed she was Jessica, and no matter what she said, Elizabeth knew she could never get her to believe she was herself.

While Jessica ran off to her next class, Elizabeth somberly gathered her books and started down the hall, blinking hard to hold back the tears that threatened to spill over onto her cheeks. Behind her, there was a burst of laughter, and somebody shouted "April Fool!"

April Fool? Elizabeth sucked in her breath.

She was beginning to wonder just exactly *who* was the April Fool.

Six

April Fools' jokes flew thick and fast at Elizabeth's lunch table. Jerry was taking everybody's picture with his squirt camera. Charlie Cashman put a plastic ice cube with a bug in the center into Lois Waller's lemonade. Then he watched with delight as Lois ran for the bathroom with her hand over her mouth. Aaron Dallas planted a rubber spider on Brooke Dennis's shoulder when she wasn't looking. When she squealed and jumped, several kids yelled, "April Fool!"

"Mind if I sit here?" Ken Matthews asked Elizabeth with a twinkle in his eye. He put his tray down on the table across from Elizabeth and her good friend, Amy Sutton. His plate was loaded with three hot dogs. He grinned at Elizabeth. "Hi, Jessica," he said.

"I'm not Jessica," Elizabeth said automatically, squirting a ribbon of yellow mustard onto her hot dog. "I'm Elizabeth." She was beginning to get a little tired of correcting everyone, and it didn't make any difference anyway. Everybody was convinced that she was Jessica *playing* Elizabeth.

Amy laughed merrily and reached for the mustard. "Listen, Jessica," she said, "when you see Elizabeth, remind her that we're going swimming tonight. And my mom said I could ask her over for dinner, too."

"That sounds great, Amy. I can't wait to show you my new pink swimsuit. And I'll be glad to come over for dinner, too."

Amy squirmed uncomfortably. "But my mom said I could only invite one person to dinner, Jessica. I've already planned on asking Elizabeth." She looked up and then pointed to the other side of the lunchroom. "Oh, there's Elizabeth now, with Mr. Davis." She stared curiously. "I wonder what they're talking about. Whatever it is, it must be funny. Mr. Davis is laughing so hard he's holding his sides."

"But that's Jessica," Elizabeth said. "Can't you see? She's wearing Jessica's clothes."

Amy gave her a sidelong look. "Ha-ha," she said. "Very funny. You can't fool me, Jessica. I've known you too long."

Elizabeth started to protest and then just gave up. It was no use. She couldn't even get her best friend to believe she wasn't Jessica. Well, later on, when it was time to go to Amy's for dinner, she would straighten everything out. Amy would definitely be surprised.

"Hey, look, Amy!" Ken suddenly shouted, standing up and pointing. "Isn't that Caroline Pearce over there in the corner with Elise? I can't believe it! Look what she's wearing. It's a new Johnny Buck T-shirt!"

"Caroline Pearce?" Amy squealed unbelievingly. She swiveled to look where Ken was pointing. "With a Johnny Buck T-shirt? You've got to be kidding!"

Caroline was a prissy, busybody sixth-grade girl who always wore her cotton blouses buttoned all the way to the collar. Elizabeth knew that she would be the last girl in the world to wear a T-shirt to school.

While Amy turned around to catch a glimpse of Caroline in a T-shirt, Ken pulled something out of his shirt pocket. It was a rubber hot dog! He yanked Amy's hot dog out of her bun and replaced it with the rubber one. Then he sat down again and tucked Amy's hot dog into one of his buns. Watching the whole thing, Elizabeth had to put both hands to her mouth to keep the giggles from escaping.

Amy turned back around. "Caroline Pearce is not wearing a T-shirt. She's got on a plain old green blouse. You must be seeing things, Ken," she said, reaching for the mustard.

Ken shrugged and winked broadly at Elizabeth. "Maybe," he admitted. "Maybe I ought to have my eyes tested. Things have been kind of blurry lately."

"Maybe you should. Anybody who could make a mistake like that *needs* glasses," Amy grumbled. After she finished putting the mustard on her hot dog, she picked it up and tried to take a bite. Then she glanced at it, turned it around, and tried to take a bite from the other end.

Elizabeth watched, trying hard not to laugh. Ken's face was red with suppressed laughter and his blue eyes shone with delight.

With a puzzled look, Amy put her hot dog down on her plate. "This hot dog is too rubbery. I can't even take a bite out of it," she complained, opening up the bun and poking it with a fork. "Leave it to our school to cook gourmet hot dogs!" she snickered.

"April fool! It's a rubber hot dog!" Ken yelled delightedly as he plucked the hot dog back out of the roll and wiped the mustard off.

For a second, Amy looked angry. But then all three of them burst into gales of laughter.

At that moment, the public-address system crackled. Over the lunchroom noise they heard the voice of Mr. Clark, the principal of Sweet Valley Middle School.

"Good afternoon," he said. He cleared his throat dramatically. "I have three *very* important announcements to make, so I must have everyone's attention." The buzz of voices in the lunchroom quieted.

"The first announcement," Mr. Clark continued, "has to do with our school buses." He paused. "I am sorry to tell you that this afternoon, those of you who ride the school buses will have to walk home. The bus drivers have gone on strike."

A collective groan was heard in the lunchroom. "Walk home?" Lois Waller moaned, pushing her brown hair away from her chubby face. "But it's over a mile!"

"Maybe you'll lose a pound or two," Jerry McAllister cut in matter-of-factly.

Alex Betner thumped Jerry on the shoulder. "Hey, look who's talking," he teased. Jerry always helped himself generously to dessert and his middle was definitely a size or two larger than anybody else's. Jerry thumped Alex back, and while everybody was still laughing, Mr. Clark spoke again.

"The second announcement is about the sixth-grade fair scheduled to be held next week."

Elizabeth put both elbows on the table and sat up expectantly. The fair was going to be a lot of fun, with booths, games, and contests for everyone. The whole class was looking forward to it.

"I'm sorry to tell all sixth-graders that the fair has to be postponed."

The second groan was even louder and longer than the first. "Postponed?" Amy asked with a blank look, turning to Elizabeth. "But how come?"

Elizabeth sat back in her seat, feeling terribly disappointed. Everybody on the planning committee had already put in a lot of work organizing the fair!

"Prepare yourselves, everybody," Mr. Clark said sadly. "The worst is yet to come."

"The worst?" Amy muttered. "What could be worse than postponing the fair?"

"The third announcement," Mr. Clark said, "is about *dessert*." He paused.

"Dessert?" Jerry asked worriedly. "What *about* dessert?"

"Our lunchroom coordinator," Mr. Clark reported, "tells me that the freezer is on the blink. All of the ice cream has melted."

The third groan was the loudest and longest of all. "Melted?" Jerry asked incredulously. "We're not going to have *any* ice cream?"

"And," he paused, "it may be a week or more before the freezer is repaired," Mr. Clark added above the hubbub of complaints and moans.

"A whole *week* without ice cream!" Jerry groaned, running his fingers through his hair. "I can't stand it!"

"That's the last of our announcements," Mr. Clark said briskly. "Except for one more." There was a sudden silence, and everybody stopped complaining to listen. Elizabeth leaned forward. The school buses, the fair, the ice cream—what more could Mr. Clark *possibly* have to tell them?

Mr. Clark cleared his throat again. "April Fool!" he said merrily.

After the shock wore off, pandemonium broke out as kids pounded each other on the back, shouting with laughter.

"I'll take *doubles* on ice cream," Jerry exclaimed, jumping up and heading for the food counter.

Lois Waller heaved an enormous sigh of relief and pushed her chair back from the table. "Thank heavens," she said. "I won't have to walk home after all!" She got up and went to the end of the lunch line for a second helping.

Elizabeth and Amy traded happy glances. "So the fair is still on for next week," Elizabeth said.

Ken stood up, the rubber hot dog sticking out of his shirt pocket. "Well, guess I'll be off," he said. He looked down at Elizabeth. "See you tonight at the party, *Jessica*." He chuckled. "Happy April Fools' Day."

Elizabeth laughed, too. In spite of the detentions and the C in cooking class, it was great to see everybody having so much fun teasing one another. After all, April Fools' Day only came once a year. And everyone would be so surprised at tonight's party, when she and Jessica told the *truth* about their great April Fools' joke!

After school that afternoon, Elizabeth looked around for Jessica, but she was nowhere to be found. Elizabeth assumed her twin had straightened things out with the Unicorns and gone off to help with their project. Anyway, she didn't have time to worry about Jessica. The first thing she had to do was to report to Mr. Davis. If she was lucky, maybe it wouldn't take too long to write the essay and then she could go to Mr. Edwards's office.

When she got to Mr. Davis's classroom, it was empty. A message was written on the blackboard: *Dear Jessica, I suddenly developed a toothache and I've gone to the dentist. We'll have to reschedule your detention for a later time. I've already fed the gerbils.* It was signed, *Mr. Davis.*

Elizabeth let out an explosive sigh of relief. It was too bad about Mr. Davis's tooth, but what a lucky break for her! One detention was out of the way, and only one to go. She hurried out of the classroom and headed down the hall—being careful not to run into Mr. Edwards's office.

"Hello," she said to Mrs. Peters, the school secretary. "I'm Elizabeth—er, Jessica Wakefield. Mr. Edwards told me to come by and help out with the filing this afternoon."

"Oh, yes, Jessica," Mrs. Peters replied, smiling over her gold-rimmed glasses. "Mr. Edwards told me. But he had to go to a meeting, and I'm afraid I have to hurry off to pick up my little boy from school. We'll have to choose another day for you to help with the filing."

Elizabeth tried not to smile, but inwardly she was rejoicing. Another lucky break! "I hope your little boy had a good April Fools' Day," she said politely.

"Thank you," Mrs. Peters said. "Are you coming to the party tonight?"

Elizabeth nodded. "Definitely. And since you don't need me, I'm going to the gym right now to help decorate."

Mrs. Peters picked up her purse and turned off the lights in the office. "Well, have fun," she said cheerfully.

Elizabeth hurried off in the direction of the gym. Things were working out much better than she had hoped! Now she could help decorate the gym with a clear conscience.

But when she got to the gym and pushed

the door open, she met Pamela Jacobson, who gave her a curious look.

"Hi, Jessica," Pamela greeted her. "What are you doing here?"

"I've come to decorate," Elizabeth said.

"But that's *Elizabeth's* job," Pamela objected. "You're not even on the committee, Jessica."

Elizabeth grinned. "I *am* Elizabeth," she said. Behind Pamela, she could see the other kids laughing and having fun. Some of them were on ladders, hanging crepe paper streamers, while others were blowing up party balloons.

Pamela put both hands on her hips. "Actually, if you want to know the truth, we're all a little mad at Elizabeth. She was supposed to be here fifteen minutes ago to help start decorating. Have you seen her anywhere?"

Elizabeth's grin faded. "But I *am* Elizabeth," she repeated. "Honest, Pamela. I would have been here on time, but I was supposed to do two detentions, one for Mr. Davis and another for Mr. Edwards."

"You see, that proves it!" Pamela exclaimed. "Elizabeth *never* has to do detention, much less *two* of them in one afternoon!"

"But it's *true!*" Elizabeth cried in protest. "Please believe me!" But she could see she was in a fix. If no one else believed her, why should Pamela?

"Listen, Jessica, everybody knows that you and Elizabeth have a super joke going, but don't you think you're overdoing it a little?" She guided Elizabeth gently toward the door. "We know that you're really Jessica, so we can't let you help. If you see Liz, tell her we're really upset that she didn't show up." With those words, she led Elizabeth out into the hall and closed the gym doors firmly.

For a minute, Elizabeth stood staring at the closed doors, wondering what to do. Her thoughts were interrupted when she spotted Lila Fowler and Ellen Riteman marching down the hall toward her. And, boy, did they look furious!

Seven

◇

"Jessica!" Lila snapped impatiently, "I *told* you that you were supposed to help us with our project this afternoon!"

Elizabeth looked wistfully at the closed gym doors, wishing she could join the kids who were working behind them. Then she squared her shoulders and looked at Lila. "Really, Lila, I'm not who you think—"

Ellen Riteman cut in impatiently. "We know, we know. You're not Jessica, right? You're Elizabeth."

Elizabeth nodded coolly. "That's right," she said.

"Well, then," Lila retorted, "if you're Elizabeth, why aren't you in the gym, working with the rest of the committee on the decorations for tonight's party?"

Elizabeth could only shrug helplessly. She began to giggle at the *logic* of Lila's response. Pamela and the others wouldn't let her decorate, because they thought she was Jessica. And Lila was convinced that she was Jessica because she wasn't decorating the gym. Of course! It was perfectly logical *and* perfectly silly at the same time. When Jessica heard all this, she was really going to flip!

Ellen nodded. "That's more like it," she said approvingly. "Come on, Jessica. You've got *work* to do." She grabbed Elizabeth by the arm.

"That's right," Lila said, grabbing the other. "Come on. We have a job for you."

"Work? A job?" That was very strange. None of the Unicorns—those girls who thought they were so rare and special—ever did any work. In fact, they spent most of their time trying to get out of committee assignments, especially the ones where they might have to pick up a hammer or a paintbrush.

"I don't understand," Elizabeth protested,

as the girls hustled her down the hall. "Where are we going?"

"The Unicorns are having a car wash," Ellen said. They went through the double doors and out onto the sidewalk in front of the school.

"A car wash?" Elizabeth asked, her eyes widening in surprise. "But the Unicorns would *never* do anything like washing cars. It's much too messy!"

Lila and Ellen exchanged amused glances. "Well, we're doing it today," Lila replied haughtily. "At the service station."

"But why are the Unicorns washing cars?" Elizabeth persisted. Other clubs at Sweet Valley Middle School held bake sales and washed cars and mowed lawns to raise money—but not the Unicorns.

"Because . . . because we need to earn money for our next party," Ellen said. She escorted Elizabeth to the service station across the street. Several Unicorns were gathered around a fancy gray Mercedes. "Hurry up, Jessica. You don't want to keep your first customer waiting."

When they got to the service station, Lila handed Elizabeth a hose and a brush. "OK,

Jessica, get to work," she commanded, gesturing in the direction of the Mercedes. "That one's all yours."

Elizabeth looked around. Janet Howell, the president of the Unicorns, was there, talking to the other members. They were all wearing their school clothes—nice, neat skirts and sweaters. Nobody was dressed for a job as wet and grubby as washing cars.

"Am I the only one who's working?" Elizabeth asked suspiciously. "Isn't anybody going to help?"

"Everyone's already done at least one car," Lila replied with a careless shrug of her shoulders. She tapped on her watch with her index finger. "Don't forget, Jessica, you were supposed to be here nearly half an hour ago."

"That's right," Ellen chirped. "We've already done our part. Now it's your turn, Jessica. Get to it!"

Elizabeth looked at the car. Of course, she could just refuse to wash it. In fact, she had half a mind to drop the hose and brush, and go home. It had been a long and tiring day, and she was just about fed up with everybody thinking she was Jessica. She was beginning to think that their April Fools' joke had worked a little too well!

But Elizabeth knew that if she refused to do what the Unicorns wanted, Jessica was bound to get in trouble with them. And while Elizabeth didn't understand why her twin thought that the Unicorns were so great, she was still fiercely loyal to Jessica. She didn't want to do anything that might jeopardize her sister's standing with her friends.

So while the Unicorns stood around and chattered noisily about boys and clothes, Elizabeth set to work on the dusty car. When she'd finished hosing it down, she washed it, then rinsed it. She tried to keep the soapy water off her freshly-washed jeans, but she wasn't very successful. By the time she finished, there were big damp spots on her jeans and blouse, her sneakers were soggy, and both her arms were aching and weary from the hard work.

Janet Howell came over to inspect the car.

"Good work," Janet said approvingly. She turned to the others. "Don't you think Jessica did a good job with the Unicorns' car wash, girls?"

"A *wonderful* job!" the Unicorns chorused.

And then, to Elizabeth's surprise, they all cried, "April Fool, Jessica!"

"April Fool?" Elizabeth turned to Lila and Ellen, her mouth dropping open. "You mean, this *wasn't* a car wash, after all?"

"Of course not, Jessica," Lila said disdainfully. "You were absolutely right when you said that a car wash is too much work for the Unicorns. It was an April Fools' joke—on you! And it was a good one, wasn't it?"

"My mother will be very pleased with the way her car looks," Ellen chimed in. "I'm really surprised, Jessica. I didn't think you'd do such a good job."

Ellen put her arm around Elizabeth's shoulders. "And you're *such* a good sport to go along with our joke without getting angry at us. Isn't she a good sport, everybody?"

All the Unicorns agreed that Jessica was indeed a good sport. Then they all decided to go to Casey's Place for ice cream. Only Elizabeth begged off, saying that she needed to go home and change her wet, grubby clothes before the party that night.

As she walked home, she thought about all the zany things that had happened to her that day. Not only had she gotten Jessica's deten-

she'd gotten Jessica's April Fools' joke as
well! She sighed wearily and rubbed her aching arms. What a day it had been. She hoped
she never had another one like it. Next year,
Jessica was just going to have to cook up a
different April Fools' joke, and that's all there
was to it!

By the time she got home, Elizabeth was
feeling a little better about the day. Enough to
laugh at the *funny* side of everything that had
happened. In the kitchen, the late-afternoon
sunlight streamed through the windows, and
the clock on the wall read four-thirty. There
was time to grab some milk and cookies before taking a quick bath and getting ready to
go to Amy's.

But Steven was already at the refrigerator.
"So *there* you are, Jess," he said, emerging
from the refrigerator with a soda can. He shook
his head, his eyes round and very solemn.
"Boy, you had better make yourself scarce,"
he warned, lowering his voice. "Mom's looking for you, and she's really on the warpath
this time."

Wearily, Elizabeth sat down on a kitchen

stool and rubbed her shoulder. "I don't suppose," she said, lifting the top off the cookie jar and taking two chocolate chip cookies, "that it would do a whole lot of good to tell you that I'm *not* Jessica."

"No, it wouldn't do any good at all," Steven said, popping the top of a cream soda can. He frowned. "But that's exactly what *I'd* say, if I were you. Right now, it would be a whole lot safer to be Elizabeth. You know, you've really messed up this time."

"Messed up?" Elizabeth asked. She leaned her elbow down on the counter and stared at Steven. This sounded serious. "What in the world has Jess done *now*?"

Steven looked at her. Then he crossed his eyes and stuck out his tongue, making a horrible face.

Elizabeth heaved a resigned sigh. "OK," she said. "What have *I* done now?"

Steven uncrossed his eyes, and took a big gulp of his cream soda. Then he reached over and grabbed one of Elizabeth's cookies right out of her hand. "Remember those plans you were supposed to mail for the Oberman project?"

Elizabeth gave Steven a serious look. "Plans?" It wouldn't help to say that she'd never *heard* of the Oberman plans. It was probably something to do with her mother's part-time interior decorating job.

"Right," Steven said, popping the cookie into his mouth. "The Oberman plans. Well, they never arrived, which means that you didn't mail them. You're in major trouble, and I mean *major*." He paused, and shook his head with a pitying look. "Boy, you couldn't pay me a million dollars to switch places with you today!"

Just then Mrs. Wakefield came into the kitchen. She was still wearing her business suit and she had a stern look on her face.

"Well, Jessica," she said, "I imagine that Steven has filled you in by now. Where have you put the Oberman plans?"

"But, Mom," Elizabeth cried, "I'm *not* Jessica! I don't know anything about any plans."

Mrs. Wakefield looked cross. "This is no time for April Fools' jokes, Jessica. I suppose you got busy with something and forgot to mail the plans. But you must have put them somewhere. Are they in your closet? Under your bed?"

Steven gave a short laugh. "If that's where they are," he said, stuffing another cookie into his mouth, "it'll take a major excavation to turn them up."

"But Mom, I'm not—" Elizabeth began, and then stopped. If her mother was convinced that she was Jessica, there wasn't a thing she could do about it. And what *had* Jessica done with the plans? Her shoulders sagged wearily. She could brush off most of the other things that had happened today, but not this. This was too important. No wonder Jessica had thought this non-switch was such a great idea!

Mrs. Wakefield looked at her watch. "It's almost five. The party is at seven, so I suggest, Jessica, that you go upstairs to your room and work on your homework for the next hour. And while you're at it, see if you can't remember what became of those plans. If you can't turn them up, I'm afraid that you'll have to come to the Town Council meeting with your father and me tonight as punishment for being so careless."

"But, Mom, I can't miss the party!" Elizabeth wailed. After all the bad things she'd suffered because people thought she was Jessica, Elizabeth just *had* to be at the party to see everybody's face when they realized that they had been fooled. And, what was she going to tell Amy about swimming and dinner?

"No buts," Mrs. Wakefield said sternly, pointing toward the door. "Upstairs, Jessica. And try to *remember!*"

Eight

◇

For the next hour, Elizabeth sat upstairs in Jessica's room, hunched over her homework. She didn't like working in Jessica's messy room, though. Dirty clothes were piled on the floor and on the unmade bed. The closet door was open, and Elizabeth could see Jessica's shoes in a tumbled heap. Over the desk, a life-size poster of Johnny Buck, Jessica's favorite rock star, smiled down at her.

Elizabeth kept worrying about the Oberman plans. She took comfort in knowing that when Jessica got home, the plans would surely be found. She was also eager to set things right by revealing her identity.

But when Jessica entered her bedroom, she plopped down on her messy bed with a delighted grin. "Wasn't today *wonderful*?" she cried happily. "Everybody was totally and absolutely fooled! It was the best joke ever!"

"That's what *you* think," Elizabeth said grimly, putting down her pencil and turning around. "What about my magazine subscription? And the detention I'm supposed to do for Mr. Davis because of the note that *you* wrote?"

Jessica shrugged. "That's the breaks, I guess," she said lightly.

"And the April Fools' joke that the Unicorns had planned for you?"

Jessica sat up, looking curious. "What April Fools' joke?" she demanded.

"The one where *I* got to wash Ellen Riteman's mother's Mercedes." Elizabeth sighed, and told Jessica the story of the Unicorns' "car wash."

When she had heard Elizabeth's tale, Jessica burst into laughter. "So you washed the *whole* car?" she asked. "While everybody stood around and watched? Oh, Elizabeth, that's a riot!"

"It depends on which end of the hose you're holding," Elizabeth said crossly. "But there's

something even more important than all that.
What about the Oberman plans? They didn't
arrive wherever they were supposed to. What
did you do with them?"

Jessica frowned. "The Oberman plans? I
mailed them the day before yesterday, just
the way I was supposed to." She looked up at
Elizabeth, her blue-green eyes wide and inno-
cent. "Honest, Elizabeth!"

Elizabeth took a deep breath. She usually
knew when Jessica was fibbing. She was pretty
sure that her twin was telling the truth this
time. "But what happened to them?" Elizabeth asked. "And what are we going to tell
Mom? She's convinced that you didn't mail
the plans. And she's threatening to make *me*
miss the party tonight if *you* don't find them.
Don't you think we ought to come clean about
this April Fools' joke?"

Jessica stood up and went to the mirror to
check her makeup. "Not on your life," she
said emphatically, adding a little touch of lip-
stick. "A bargain's a bargain, Elizabeth. We
agreed to do this non-switch until the party
tonight. As far as I'm concerned, that's exactly what we're going to do."

"But it's not fair!" Elizabeth exclaimed indignantly. "If you don't find those plans, Mom says I have to go to the Town Council meeting with her and Dad tonight! I'll be taking *your* punishment."

"That's really too bad," Jessica said regretfully. "But I'll bet the family will get an even bigger laugh when they hear the truth and know how much they've been fooled. Mom will probably even want to do something extranice for you to make up for the punishment." Her eyes twinkled mischievously. "And just *think* of the terrific stories you'll have to tell at school tomorrow! And anyway," Jessica added calmly, passing a comb through her blond hair, "Mom probably wouldn't believe us if we told her. She'd just think I was trying to get out of something, that's all. No, it's better if we leave things just as they are."

Elizabeth stared at Jessica with a mixture of anger and disappointment. She felt Jessica was *using* her by not taking responsibility for the trouble and unhappiness she was causing. How could her own sister totally disregard her feelings? Elizabeth bit her lip.

Jessica didn't even notice how hurt Elizabeth felt. She simply tossed her blond hair over her shoulder and dropped the comb on the dresser.

"And about the subscription—well, you know how that happened," she said, turning around. "If I'd put down your mystery magazine, Mr. Davis would have guessed our joke and our whole day would have been ruined." She reached out and patted Elizabeth's hand. "Don't worry, Lizzie. If you read about rock music, maybe you'll start to enjoy it more!"

She bounced to the door, where she turned around with a grin. "See you later," she said with a careless wave.

Elizabeth turned back to her homework, but everything looked blurry as she blinked back tears. She could hear Jessica downstairs in the kitchen laughing with her mother and Steven. The joke had gone far enough, Elizabeth decided resentfully. In fact, it had gone much too far! She was through playing this silly April Fools' game.

But before Elizabeth had time to act, the front doorbell rang.

"Hi, Mrs. Wakefield," Amy said. "Is Elizabeth here?"

"Yes. She's in the kitchen with Steven, eating some cookies. Why don't you join them?"

"I hope she hasn't eaten too *many* cookies," Amy said. "We're supposed to go for a quick swim and then eat dinner at my house before the party."

"That's a good idea. Just make sure Steven watches you," Mrs. Wakefield said. "I'm on my way out. Jessica," she called upstairs. "Do you want anything from the drugstore?"

"No, thanks," Elizabeth replied dully. After her mother closed the front door, she heard Jessica's voice in the hall.

"Hi, Amy."

"Hi," Amy said. "I've been trying to catch you all day. Did Jessica tell you about the plans for this evening? After we go swimming, my mom says we can have dinner over at my house."

"But I'm not Elizabeth," Jessica replied. "I'm Jessica."

Upstairs, Elizabeth bent forward, listening. Maybe, if Jessica tried just a little harder, Amy would believe her. Of all the people in the world, Amy ought to be able to tell the difference between them. After all, Amy was her best friend!

Amy giggled. "You can drop the joke, Elizabeth," she said. "Remember me? I'm your best friend. I know that you and your twin are doubles, but if anybody can tell the difference between you, it's me."

Elizabeth sighed sorrowfully.

Amy giggled again. "Well, then, *Jessica*," she said spiritedly, "since Elizabeth has stood me up, the two of us might as well go swimming together."

"Well," Jessica said, "since you put it that way, we might as well."

Elizabeth heard her twin come upstairs and go into her bedroom. She opened Jessica's door a crack and was shocked to see Jessica pulling a sweatshirt over *her* brand-new bathing suit. What right did Jessica have to skip out on what should have been her punishment, *and* to wear Elizabeth's brand-new swimsuit?

Elizabeth sat down with a thump on the chair. She had never felt more miserable.

When the telephone rang a few minutes later, she heard her father's voice out in the hall, answering it.

"Elizabeth Wakefield? No, I'm sorry, she's busy tonight."

"Dad," Elizabeth called, getting up. "Was that for me?"

"No, *Jessica*," her father said pointedly, "it was for Elizabeth. It was Carson Stable. The girl who's been exercising Thunder didn't show up tonight, and they wanted to know if Liz could spend an hour with him. But since she's swimming with Amy, they'll have to find somebody else."

Elizabeth sank back down on the chair with a heavy groan.

Nine

◇

At six, Mrs. Wakefield knocked on the door of Jessica's room and came in.

"Well, Jessica," she asked, "have you re-membered what you did with those plans?"

Elizabeth shook her head.

"I'll spare you the lecture on responsibil-ity," Mrs. Wakefield said. "But you're coming to the Council Meeting with your father and me tonight."

Elizabeth looked pleadingly at her mother. "Couldn't you please change your mind?" she asked in a small voice. "There's an extra-special reason that I want to go to the party."

Mrs. Wakefield smiled and gently stroked Elizabeth's hair. "I understand, dear," she said. "You haven't had a good day, have you?"

Elizabeth sighed, longing to tell her mother everything. But it wouldn't help. Her mother would only think she was Jessica, trying to get sympathy. "No," she replied. "I guess I haven't."

"Well, tomorrow's bound to be better," her mother said cheerfully. "As for tonight, why don't you change for the Council Meeting?" She gestured toward Jessica's closet, where her new pink-and-white dress was hanging on the door. "Why don't you wear that dress?"

Elizabeth sucked in her breath. "I don't want to wear that dress!" she burst out angrily. And then, in a quieter voice, she said, "I think I'll wear one of Elizabeth's dresses, if you don't think she'd mind."

Her mother stood up, smiling. "No, I'm sure she wouldn't," she said. "Wear whatever you like." She paused near the door. "By the way," she said, "the Council is meeting in the library at the Middle School."

Dumbfounded, Elizabeth stared at her mother. It was bad enough having to miss the party, but now she would have to walk right past the gym, where she would hear everybody having a good time. And even worse, some of the kids might *see* her!

Elizabeth's spirits were so low that she decided to wear her favorite blue dress with the lace collar. She tied her hair with a blue ribbon, and fastened her new gold charm bracelet with the little dancing horses on her wrist. When she looked at herself in the mirror, Elizabeth managed a wan smile. Her cheerful appearance certainly didn't reveal how terrible she felt.

Except for Mr. Wakefield humming a tuneless little melody, the ride to the school was silent. As they parked in the darkened school parking lot, Elizabeth kept her fingers crossed that she wouldn't see any of her friends. But as they walked up the sidewalk, she bumped into Julie Porter, a good friend who worked with her on *The Sweet Valley Sixers.*

"Oh, hi, Jessica," Julie said. "I've been looking everywhere for Elizabeth. Do you know where she is?" Her voice became urgent. "There's something really important about the paper that I have to talk over with her."

"But *I'm* Elizabeth," Elizabeth protested. "You can talk it over with me."

On either side of her, her father and mother laughed. "It *is* April Fools' Day, you know, Julie," her mother said.

"I know, Mrs. Wakefield," Julie replied. "Listen, if you see Elizabeth, will you tell her there's an emergency problem with the latest issue of *The Sixers*? We need her to tell us what to do."

"What is it?" Elizabeth asked worriedly. When she had looked at the paper the day before, everything had seemed just fine. What could have gone wrong? "Tell me. Maybe I can help."

Julie laughed merrily. "How could *you* help with *The Sixers*, Jessica?" she exclaimed. "You don't even know how to type!"

Mr. Wakefield chuckled. "We'll be sure that Elizabeth gets your message," he called as Julie ran off toward the gym.

Mrs. Wakefield put her hand on Mr. Wakefield's arm. "Ned," she said. "Don't you think we'd better get to the meeting? We don't want to be late."

When they entered the school, Elizabeth was surprised to see her parents head for the gym.

"Where are we going?" she asked, turning to catch up with her parents.

Mrs. Wakefield held up a small paper bag. "We have an errand," she said. "Elizabeth phoned just before we left the house. She spilled punch on her shirt at Amy's house, so she asked us to bring her another one to change into. We'll just swing by the gym before we go to the meeting. Will you find your sister and give her this fresh shirt?"

Elizabeth couldn't believe her ears. She was going to have to walk right into the middle of the party and then leave again with her parents waiting for her right outside the door. Everybody would see her!

She caught her mother's arm. "Please," she begged, "can't *you* take the shirt into the gym and let *me* wait outside?"

Mrs. Wakefield smiled down at her. "But what would the kids think?" she asked. "They don't want a couple of old-fogey parents crashing their party." She shook her head and handed the bag to Elizabeth. "No, you go in, dear. We'll wait right here at the door for you."

So, with her heart beating fast, Elizabeth opened the door. She might as well get it over with as quickly as possible.

The gym was crowded with kids in a party mood. Everyone was all dressed up, and the gym looked great. Crepe paper streamers were draped everywhere, and masses of colorful balloons hung from the ceiling. Somebody had put a tape player and a stack of tapes on a table in one corner, and in another, Mrs. Gerhart and some of the girls were setting a table for cookies and punch. The table was decorated with a huge bouquet of pretty flowers.

Elizabeth looked around, wishing that *she* could be helping to fill the punch bowl or set out the cookies. But she couldn't. She had to go sit through a boring Town Council meeting with her parents—and all because of the silly April Fools' joke she and Jessica had planned. She wished with all her heart that she had never agreed to such a wacky scheme.

Out in the middle of the floor, Elizabeth caught sight of Jessica talking with Mr. Davis and some of the kids from their homeroom. Hurrying to get her errand over with, Elizabeth made her way through the crowd toward them.

"Jessica," she said. "I've brought your shirt."

Suddenly the others all stepped back, and

Elizabeth found herself alone with Jessica in the middle of a big circle. Everybody else stood around the edge, watching and giggling.

"I'm glad you're here," Jessica said with a big smile.

"Well, *I'm* not," Elizabeth said, a dull red flush creeping up her cheeks. Why was everybody watching them? "Anyway, I can't stay. I've got to go." Handing Jessica the bag, she turned to leave.

"Wait!" Jessica called after her. "Where are you going?" Somewhere in the circle, one of the kids snickered.

Elizabeth gave her twin a dirty look. It wasn't fair to ask her a question like that in front of the whole class. "You know where I'm going," she said rebelliously. "To the Town Council meeting with Mom and Dad, that's where."

"No, you aren't," Mrs. Wakefield said, stepping forward.

Elizabeth whirled around. "You mean, I don't have to come to the meeting with you?"

"That's right, *Elizabeth*," her father said with a smile. "You can stay at the party." His smile widened into a grin. "Actually, I think it's *your* party."

Elizabeth looked around, shaking her head

in confusion. *Her* party? "But I don't understand—" she began.

"April Fool, Elizabeth!" Jessica shouted happily.

"April Fool, Elizabeth!" her mother and father shouted.

"April Fool, Elizabeth!" the whole class shouted.

Ten

Elizabeth stared openmouthed at the circle of friendly, laughing kids that surrounded her. "April Fool?" she gulped.

"Yes. You were fooled, weren't you?" Jessica said proudly. "The whole thing was an April Fools' joke. It was all my idea." She grinned with self-satisfaction. "It was the best joke anybody's ever dreamed up." When Elizabeth didn't say anything, her look became anxious. "You're not angry with me, are you?"

Elizabeth shook her head, stunned and almost speechless. All the ridiculous stuff that had happened that day—the detentions, the

C in cooking class, the Unicorns' car wash, the Oberman papers. How much of it had been *real*, and how much had been part of Jessica's crazy joke? "I—I don't know what to say," she said unsteadily. "I'm still not sure what's going on."

"That's all right," Jessica said comfortingly. "You don't really have to say anything." Then she leaned over and took the bouquet of flowers off the table and handed it to Elizabeth. "Here you are, Lizzie. You get the Good Sport of the Year Award, from all of us! Congratulations." Then everybody began to clap loudly.

"Yay, Elizabeth!" Amy shouted. "Way to go!"

Holding her flowers, Elizabeth looked around at her friends, her teachers, and her family, all laughing and clapping. "You mean," she demanded, "that all of you were in on the joke the whole time?"

Mrs. Wakefield stepped forward, smiling. "Your father and Steven and I helped organize the plan," she said.

Jessica nodded happily. "Do you remember when we were scheming yesterday afternoon, out under the pine tree, and I suddenly remembered I had to tell Mom something?"

"What she had to tell me," Mrs. Wakefield said, "was that you'd agreed to her April Fools' idea—which was really a joke on *you!*"

Elizabeth nodded, beginning to piece things together so that they made sense. "So all that stuff about Jessica losing the Oberman plans—"

"It was all part of the joke," her mother admitted. She looked a little concerned. "We had to be convincing so that you'd fall for it. But I certainly hope we didn't carry it too far, honey." She touched Elizabeth's hand. "We weren't too hard on you, were we?"

Elizabeth thought about the hour she had spent in Jessica's room, doing her homework and feeling unhappy. "I guess not," she said, with a rueful little laugh. "I got my social studies map done, so the time wasn't wasted. But I missed a chance to exercise Thunder."

Mr. Wakefield threw back his head and laughed. "No, you didn't, Elizabeth," he said. "You didn't miss a thing. That phone call wasn't from Carson Stable. It was only Steven calling from the other phone. It was just another part of the joke."

Elizabeth breathed an enormous sigh of relief. "So the stable wasn't looking for me after all," she exclaimed.

"No," her father said. "But someone from the stable had called a little earlier and asked if you'd be free on Saturday morning to give Thunder a workout. That's what gave me the idea. Can you do it on Saturday?"

Elizabeth's eyes lit up and she agreed happily. There wasn't anything she liked better to do on Saturdays than to ride Thunder.

"And you didn't miss dinner at my house, either, Elizabeth," Amy said, smiling broadly. "Jessica and I came over to the school to help Mrs. Gerhart and some of the others ice your cake."

Elizabeth gulped back her surprise. "My *cake*? What cake?"

"That cake," Mrs. Gerhart said, pointing to a large delicious-looking cake. Its blue-and-white frosting spelled out "April Fool, Elizabeth!" in huge swirling letters.

"We wanted to bake it in cooking class today," Mrs. Gerhart went on, "but we couldn't take a chance that you'd see it and figure out what was going on." Her eyes twinkled. "So we did soufflés instead. And I must say, Elizabeth, your soufflé was simply *beautiful*, one of the very best I've ever seen in all my years of teaching. It really deserved the A I put down in my grade book beside your name, once class was over."

Jessica leaned forward. "And she's even going to let me do a makeup on my soufflé, Lizzie," she whispered confidentially. "I'm sure I can do a better job when I really put my mind to it. Next time I'll be sure not to slam the oven door!"

Mr. Davis stepped forward. His eyebrows were pulled together sternly. "About the detention you're supposed to make up, Elizabeth—"

Elizabeth looked up nervously. But Mr. Davis's eyes were twinkling.

"You mean, the detention was part of the joke, too?" she asked. "The note you showed me wasn't real, after all?"

"Well, not exactly," Jessica muttered, looking down at the floor. Her cheeks had turned a bright pink. "I mean—that is—"

"What Jessica means," Mr. Davis explained gently, "is that the note she wrote *was* real. But during homeroom this morning, I really *did* expect you two girls to change places, so I was completely taken in by your non-switch. That's why I asked Jessica to come up and get your award. And that's why I assigned *you*

the detention, Elizabeth. I thought you were
Jessica, pretending to be Elizabeth." He laughed.
"You see? You two really had me completely
fooled."

"But we straightened it all out at lunch-
time," Jessica chimed in, "when I let Mr. Davis
in on the joke. He agreed to change the magazine order form. So you'll get that mystery
magazine you wanted." She grinned. "You
won't have to read a year's worth of *Teen Rock*
after all, Lizzie!"

Mr. Davis nodded. "And since the note I
showed you was real, Jessica has agreed that
the only fair thing is for her to serve the
detention, later this week." He grinned. "As
you might guess, I didn't have a toothache
after all. It was just a way of letting us both
off the hook."

"And because you were running in the hallway after Mr. Davis kept you late, Elizabeth,"
Mr. Edwards spoke up, "I've decided to over-
look the detention I assigned to you." He
turned to give Jessica a pointed glance. "Especially after your sister promised that she would
never run in the hallways again, *and* after she
volunteered to spend a half hour helping Mrs.
Peters catch up with the filing."

Elizabeth stared at her twin. Jessica was going to do all that? What a surprise!

Jessica tossed her head self-consciously. "I know that you think I'm kind of selfish sometimes, Lizzie. But I don't always *mean* to be. Honest." She grinned crookedly. "I just wanted this to be a really *good* April Fools' joke. Some things happened that I didn't exactly plan for. And maybe it *did* get a little out of hand, especially toward the end." She glanced down at the bag that Elizabeth had given her. "What's in here?"

"It's your shirt," Elizabeth replied. "Mom said we were bringing it because you wanted to change."

Lila Fowler now stepped forward and took the bag out of Jessica's hand. She opened it and looked inside.

"But this isn't a shirt at all," she said to Jessica. "It's your purple Unicorn scarf!" And she held it up for everyone to see.

"I think," Lila said dramatically, "that we ought to let Elizabeth wear it for tonight." She stepped forward and tied it loosely around Elizabeth's neck. "After all, she did such a good job washing Mrs. Riteman's car this afternoon, she ought to have *something* to show for all her work. And for being such a good sport, too."

Elizabeth gently fingered Jessica's purple scarf.

"I hereby declare," Lila went on in a loud voice, "that Elizabeth Wakefield is an honorary Unicorn for one day every year—on April Fools' Day!" All the Unicorns clapped. A few of the boys who thought the Unicorns were silly gave a hiss and a boo.

Elizabeth laughed. She had never wanted to belong to the Unicorns, and it wasn't any secret that she thought they were snobs. But it probably wouldn't hurt to be a Unicorn for one day a year, especially on April Fools' Day.

She turned to Jessica. "Did you know that Lila and Ellen were going to make me wash Mrs. Riteman's car?" she asked. "Was that something you set up, too?"

Jessica's eyes were twinkling. "Of course," she crowed. "I thought that was one of the very *best* parts of the joke!"

Elizabeth stared at her twin, wondering whether she should hug her or *strangle* her! There weren't any detentions, or punishments, or a C in cooking class. But she'd been pretty uncomfortable most of the day, trying to figure out how to cope with the crazy things that had happened.

She cleared her throat. "Uh, Jess," she said, "there's one thing that happened this afternoon that I forgot to tell you about."

"There is?" Jessica asked eagerly. "Another part of the joke, you mean?" Everybody fell silent to hear what Elizabeth was going to say.

Elizabeth shook her head. "Not exactly," she said. "Actually, this afternoon I was really mad at you because of all the things that were happening. I decided to get even by playing along with everybody who thought I was Jessica. So when Bruce Patman called to ask me if you'd go with him to the next Johnny Buck concert—"

"Bruce Patman called?" Jessica squealed excitedly. "Oh, Lizzie, that's terrific!" She threw a triumphant look at Lila and Ellen, who exchanged envious glances. All the Unicorns thought that Bruce Patman was the cutest boy in seventh grade. "So what did you tell him?"

Elizabeth shrugged and looked down at her bouquet of flowers. "Oh, not much, really," she said. "Just that he is a stuck-up snob and that I never wanted to speak to him again as long as I lived."

Jessica's mouth dropped open and a look of horror spread across her face. "Oh, Elizabeth," she wailed. "You *didn't*! This is awful! How can I ever face Bruce again!"

Elizabeth couldn't keep a straight face any longer. "April Fool!" she cried, laughing.

Jessica stared at her, her eyes wide. "Bruce *didn't* call. You *didn't* say any of that to him?"

Elizabeth flung her arms around her twin and hugged her. "No," she admitted cheerfully. "He didn't. And I didn't." She gave Jessica a stern look. "But after all the grief you put me through, maybe I *should*!"

Jessica hugged her twin. As the circle broke up and everybody headed for the refreshment table, Mr. and Mrs. Wakefield left for their meeting.

"Race you for the first piece of cake," Jessica cried. As Elizabeth followed her twin, she was sure that this was the very best April Fools' Day ever.

Eleven

"Well, Elizabeth," Amy said, as the two girls carried their trays to a table in the cafeteria, "are you glad that April Fools' Day is over and you can go back to being your old self again?"

Elizabeth pulled out a chair and sat down. "You bet," she said. "My life may not have as much excitement as Jessica's, but if I ever consider being Jessica again—or even consider being Jessica pretending to be Elizabeth—please shut me in a closet and don't let me come out for an entire week!" She grinned. "Not even for meals!"

Amy nodded in agreement. "Jessica is a lot of fun, but she sure gets into a lot of scrapes."

Julie Porter came up, carrying a sandwich in a brown paper bag. "Room for one more, Elizabeth?" she asked. She leaned closer, peering down at Elizabeth. "It is you, isn't it?" she asked anxiously.

Elizabeth laughed. "It's me," she replied. "Honest. By the way, what was the emergency with *The Sixers* that you were talking about last night, Julie? I looked for you during the party to ask you about it, but I couldn't find you anywhere."

Julie looked embarrassed. "Oh, there *isn't* any emergency after all."

"You mean, it was all part of Jessica's joke?" Elizabeth asked.

"No, not really," Julie replied, sitting down. "I mean, I thought there was a problem when I saw you last night. But we managed to solve it this morning."

"That's good. What was the problem?"

Julie opened her carton of milk, stuck in her straw, and took a sip. "Remember the list of eight booths for the fair that Mr. Bowman gave us?"

Elizabeth nodded. Mr. Bowman was their

English teacher. He was helping the sixth-graders organize a fair that was going to be held the Saturday after next to raise money for field trips. "He told us we could print the list just the way he gave it to us."

"Right," Julie agreed. "Except that it *wasn't* the final list. There are really ten booths. He left off two—the water balloon booth and the Wheel of Fortune. And retyping the list meant that we had to change the whole layout of the page. But we got it done this morning."

Jessica, Lila, and Ellen stopped by the table and heard what Julie was saying. "What about a Wheel of Fortune?" Jessica asked curiously.

"Oh, you know, Jessica," Ellen told her, "there'll be someone dressed up like a gypsy fortune-teller spinning a wheel around. Maybe I'll ask Mr. Bowman if I can sign up for that booth. It might be a lot of fun."

Jessica tossed her long blond hair over her shoulder. "But *you* don't have long hair, El-len," she replied. "How can you be a gypsy if you don't have long hair?" She thought for a minute. "Mom's got a floor-length peasant dress that I used as a Halloween costume once. I know it would make a great gypsy outfit. I could wear lots of gold jewelry—

necklaces, bracelets, and dangling earrings."
She sighed happily. "I'd look absolutely terrific, don't you think?"

"But *your* hair is blond, Jessica," Lila pointed
out haughtily. "Gypsies have dark hair," she
said as she patted her long brown hair. "I
really think *I* ought to do the Wheel of Fortune. I'm sure my father would be glad to buy
me a *new* dress that would be perfect for it."
Lila's father was one of the wealthier men in
Sweet Valley and he was always buying her
new clothes.

Elizabeth laughed. "Well, you'll just have
to wait until Monday to see who gets which
booth. Mr. Bowman is going to hold a drawing to make sure that all the jobs are handed
out fairly."

Julie laughed. "Yeah. It has to be done that
way because there are booths that no one
would ever pick. The water balloon toss is a
real dud. Who'd want to sit and have kids
throw water balloons at them all day long?"
She made a face. "Some of them might even
have good aim!"

Jessica shuddered. "Well, that's one job I
definitely wouldn't take," she muttered. She
could imagine how her clothes and hair would

look after being hit with a couple of water balloons.

Lila glanced at her watch. "We've got to get going," she said. "There's a Unicorn meeting in a few minutes." Lila walked off with Jessica and Ellen.

Amy looked at Elizabeth. "Which booth are you hoping to get?"

"None of them, actually," Elizabeth said, digging into her salad. "I'm going to help Olivia with the posters. It's a job that will keep us busy right up to the time of the fair. What about you? Are you going to be in the drawing for one of the booths?"

Amy nodded her head emphatically. "I wouldn't miss it for the world," she said. "I'm really looking forward to the fair. It's going to be the best thing the sixth-graders have done all year."

Elizabeth agreed. The fair was going to be great!

Who will get the best booth at the sixth grade fair? Find out in Sweet Valley Twins #29, **Jessica and the Brat Attack.**

SWEET VALLEY TWINS

These are the stories about Jessica and Elizabeth when they are just twelve years old, as all the Sweet Valley excitement begins.

☐	BEST FRIENDS #1	15655/$2.75
☐	TEACHER'S PET #2	15656/$2.75
☐	THE HAUNTED HOUSE #3	15657/$2.75
☐	CHOOSING SIDES #4	15658/$2.75
☐	SNEAKING OUT #5	15659/$2.75
☐	THE NEW GIRL #6	15660/$2.75
☐	THREE'S A CROWD #7	15661/$2.75
☐	FIRST PLACE #8	15662/$2.75
☐	AGAINST THE RULES #9	15676/$2.75
☐	ONE OF THE GANG #10	15677/$2.75
☐	BURIED TREASURE #11	15692/$2.75
☐	KEEPING SECRETS #12	15538/$2.50
☐	STRETCHING THE TRUTH #13	15654/$2.75
☐	TUG OF WAR #14	15663/$2.75
☐	THE OLDER BOY #15	15664/$2.75
☐	SECOND BEST #16	15665/$2.75
☐	BOYS AGAINST GIRLS #17	15666/$2.75
☐	CENTER OF ATTENTION #18	15668/$2.75
☐	THE BULLY #19	15667/$2.75
☐	PLAYING HOOKY #20	15606/$2.75
☐	LEFT BEHIND #21	15609/$2.75
☐	OUT OF PLACE #22	15628/$2.75
☐	CLAIM TO FAME #23	15624/$2.75
☐	JUMPING TO CONCLUSIONS #24	15635/$2.75
☐	STANDING OUT #25	15653/$2.75
☐	TAKING CHARGE #26	15669/$2.75

Buy them at your local bookstore or use this page to order:

- -

Bantam Books, Dept. SVT3, 414 East Golf Road, Des Plaines, IL 60016

Please send me the books I have checked above. I am enclosing $_____ (please add $2.00 to cover postage and handling). Send check or money order—no cash or C.O.D.s please.

Mr/Ms _____

Address _____

City/State _____ Zip _____

SVT3—2/89

Please allow four to six weeks for delivery. This offer expires 8/89.
Prices and availability subject to change without notice.

THE CLASS TRIP

SWEET VALLEY TWINS SUPER EDITION #1

Join Jessica and Elizabeth in the very first SWEET VALLEY TWINS Super Edition—it's longer, can be read out of sequence, and is full of page-turning excitement!

The day of the big sixth-grade class trip to the Enchanted Forest is finally here! But Jessica and Elizabeth have a fight and spend the beginning of the trip arguing. When Elizabeth decides to make up, Jessica has disappeared. In a frantic search for her sister, Elizabeth finds herself in a series of dangerous and exciting Alice In Wonderland-type of adventures.

☐ 15588-1 $2.95/$3.50 in Canada

Buy it at your local bookstore or use this page to order.

Special Offer
Buy a Bantam Book
for only 50¢.

Now you can order the exciting books you've
been wanting to read straight from Bantam's
latest catalog of hundreds of titles. *And* this
special offer gives you the opportunity to purchase
a Bantam book for only 50¢. Here's how:

By ordering any five books at the regular
price per order, you can also choose any other
single book listed (up to a $5.95 value) for only
50¢. Some restrictions do apply, so for further
details send for Bantam's catalog of titles today.

Just send us your name and address and
we'll send you Bantam Book's SHOP AT
HOME CATALOG!